Don't count the number of birthdays. Count how happy you feel. I'm Birthday Bear, and I'll help make your birthdays the best ever.

I'm Wish Bear, and if you wish on my star, maybe your special dream will come true.

If you're ever feeling lonely, just call on me, Friend Bear. See, I've got a daisy for you and a daisy for me.

Grr! I'm Grumpy Bear. There's a cloud on my tummy to show that I take the grouchies away, so you can be happy again.

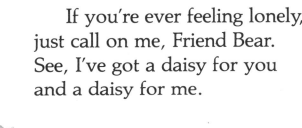

I'm Love-a-Lot Bear. I have two hearts on my tummy. One is for you; the other is for someone you love.

It's my job to bring you sweet dreams. I'm Bedtime Bear, and right now I'm a bit sleepy. Are you sleepy, too?

Now that you know all of us, we hope that you'll have a special place for us in your heart, just like we do for you.

With love from all of us,

The Care Bears

Care Bears, Care Bears Logo, Tenderheart Bear, Friend Bear, Grumpy Bear, Birthday Bear, Cheer Bear, Bedtime Bear, Funshine
Bear, Love-a-Lot
Bear, Wish Bear and Good Luck Bear are trademarks of American Greetings Corporation, Parker Brothers, authorized user.

Library of Congress Cataloging in Publication Data: Johnson, Ward. Caring is what counts. SUMMARY: The Care Bears join forces to
save a young runaway from the clutches of Professor Coldheart who wants everybody to lose their feelings.
[1. Emotions—Fiction] I. Cooke, Tom, ill.
II. Title. PZ7.J6394Car 1983 [E] 83-2394 ISBN 0-910313-05-9
Manufactured in Hong Kong.   2 3 4 5 6 7 8 9 0

A Tale from the

Care Bears

Caring is What Counts

Story by Ward Johnson
Pictures by Tom Cooke

Things were buzzing in the land of Care-a-lot.
All the Care Bears were discussing which one of them
would be voted Bear of the Week.

Funshine Bear, who always said something good
about everyone, did a little dance, waved her arms
and said, "Oh, I just know that it will be Birthday
Bear."

Birthday Bear looked up from the new joke he was writing and smiled.

"I don't think any of us deserve to win," Grumpy Bear growled. "None of us did anything really special this week."

"Don't be such a silly old grump," laughed Tenderheart Bear as he slid down a rainbow. "Each one of us is special in one way or another, and we all helped someone this week. Even you, Grumpy, although you don't like to admit it."

Friend Bear added, "I know who deserves the award most this week. Bedtime Bear. He helped Sally get over her fear of the dark. Isn't that right, Bedtime . . . Bedtime?"

But Bedtime Bear wasn't listening. He had fallen asleep on a comfortable cloud.

They were interrupted by the Caretaker, who suddenly stopped shining a rainbow and called out, "I think I hear someone crying. Care Bear alert! Care Bear alert!"

Whenever the Care Bears heard those words, they knew that they were *really* needed.

They all ran to the edge of their clouds and looked
out to see why the Care Bear alert had sounded.

They saw a boy and a girl standing on a street
corner. The boy looked angry and the girl was crying.

"Please don't go, Kevin," the girl sobbed. "You won't solve anything by running away."

Kevin answered, "I've got to get away, Donna. My parents don't understand me. They hurt my feelings, and now they want to move to a strange new town. I won't go. I'll run away first."

"Kevin, you know sometimes friends can help when you feel that no one else understands," Donna answered. "If you talk to me, maybe I can help you to feel better."

Kevin gave a sad smile. "Thanks, Donna, but I've made up my mind. I'm going to some place where no one can make me feel bad anymore."

Kevin turned and ran down the block. When he reached the corner, he waved briefly to Donna and then was gone.

"Oh, Kevin, please be careful," Donna called after him.

Friend Bear turned to the others. "It looks like Donna needs the help of a Caring Bear. Who will help her?"

"I will!" shouted all the other Bears at once.

"Well, then, let's all go," said Funshine Bear. And they did.

Donna was sitting on her front stoop, staring sadly into space, when she noticed that she was surrounded by a group of small Bears. "Who are you?" she asked.

"We're the Care Bears and we've come from Care-a-lot to help you let Kevin know that he can't harden his heart and run away from his problems," Good Luck Bear replied.

"Oh, thank you," Donna said. "Can you help me find him and bring him back?"

"Well, we're not here to bake cookies," growled Grumpy Bear. "Let's get going!"

While the Care Bears were talking to Donna, Kevin made his way across the city to a rusty gateway that opened on a large park. Kevin was thirsty, and he saw a water fountain sparkling in the park. He went inside to get a drink, but he soon noticed that it was not a very nice place. The plants and flowers drooped and the grass under his feet was dry and brown.

Before he could walk to the fountain he heard a screechy voice say, "I see you've come for a drink from my wonderful fountain, and it looks to me like—you'll do."

Kevin looked around and saw an odd-looking man
walking toward him.

"I'll do for what?" asked Kevin, suddenly afraid.

"First of all let me introduce myself," said the man.
"My name is Professor Coldheart, M.S."

"What does the M.S. stand for?" Kevin asked.

"Mad scientist, of course," said Coldheart.

"What do you do that's so mad?" Kevin asked timidly.

"Nothing, really. Oh, I do have a new plan to solve everyone's problems, and some *stupid people* think it's crazy. I'll show you how it works. Here, pinch this; go ahead. Don't be afraid." And with that Professor Coldheart held out his arm.

Kevin did what he was told and pinched it.

"Didn't feel a thing," said Coldheart. "Good thing,
too. Because otherwise you might have hurt me. Then
I might have gotten angry. As it was I felt nothing.
Isn't it grand? If you never feel anything, you can
never feel angry or sad."

"But," said Kevin, "you never feel happy either."

Coldheart, however, wasn't listening. Instead he strolled over to the fountain and got Kevin a glass of shimmering, cool water.

"Here, drink this," Professor Coldheart said. "It will make you feel better, not so angry with your mother and father."

"How did you know about them?" Kevin asked.

"Oh, we scientists know a good deal about many things," the mad scientist said smoothly.

Kevin was feeling so bad inside, and Coldheart seemed so sure of himself, that Kevin reached out, took the glass and drank the water. It felt icy cold as it went down his throat, and he could feel himself getting less angry. Soon he didn't feel sad when he thought of moving to a new town. Finally he didn't feel anything at all.

Coldheart reached out and pinched Kevin.
The boy didn't even notice.

"Aha!" cried the mad scientist. "I knew that my
formula would work. Soon I will have everybody in
the world not feeling a thing!"

Just as Kevin finished swallowing the water, the
Care Bears arrived at the park.

"Oh dear," said Tenderheart Bear, peering through
the gate. "What will we do? It looks as if Kevin will
never feel anything again."

"And what is worse," said Cheer Bear, "is that
soon Professor Coldheart may have everyone in the
world not feeling or loving any more. And we all
know that caring is what counts."

"For goodness' sake," grumbled Grumpy Bear. "When was the last time we Care Bears ever failed to help? One of us will have to go and rescue Kevin, that's all."

"But who will go?" asked Birthday Bear. "The thought of it makes me feel like a party without ice cream."

"Why don't you go, Grumpy?" asked Funshine Bear.

"What a terrible idea," growled Grumpy Bear.

"All right then," sighed Friend Bear. "I guess you shouldn't go."

"That's even a worse idea," said Grumpy, and he floated up and over the gates to the park. He was soon standing next to Coldheart.

"Oh," said Coldheart, "are you also here to drink my wonderful formula?"

"I certainly am not," said Grumpy Bear. "That formula is an awful idea. It will never help anyone enjoy life."

Coldheart laughed and then said in a very nasty voice, "What do you know? You're only a silly, little, blue bear." And Coldheart pushed Grumpy Bear away with one of his long, cold fingers.

Now this was the first time in his life that Grumpy Bear had ever been laughed at, and he started to feel all sad inside.

Coldheart could see that Grumpy Bear was feeling sad, so he whispered smoothly, "You'd feel ever so much better if you took a drink from my fountain. Go ahead . . . go ahead."

When Friend Bear saw what was happening, he cried, "Care Bear emergency alert!" And with that all the other Care Bears, bringing Donna with them, floated over the gates and into the park.

When he saw them approaching, Coldheart said icily, "Who asked you to come in? Scat! Get lost!"

"Now wait one minute," said Love-a-lot. "We're not going to let you make the world into a place where nobody has any feelings."

"Try and stop me," sneered Coldheart. "I've got Kevin in my power and soon everyone will want my formula."

"We'll see about that," said Wish Bear. "Kevin, think about a time when your wish came true. How did it make you feel?" But Kevin just stared straight ahead.

The other Bears soon realized what Wish Bear was trying to do. If they could get Kevin to show some sign of feeling, Coldheart's power over him would be broken.

"Hey, Kevin, here's a good one," said Birthday Bear. "What's green, has a stem and lives in Care-a-lot? A Care Pear! Get it?"

But Kevin did not crack a smile.

For one short minute the Care Bears began to get discouraged.

Then Good Luck Bear took a deep breath and called, "Care Bears, line up!" All the Bears stood in front of Kevin. "Now, Kevin, really look at us."

Kevin turned, and when he saw all those pictures
on ten fat little Bear tummies, he began to feel some
warmth in his heart.

"Oh, Kevin," Donna said. "I think that you are
going to smile. I'm so glad because I do like you so."
Donna reached out and took Kevin's hand.

When Donna touched Kevin, something
wonderful began to happen in the park. Slowly the
trees began to turn green again, and new grass began
to push its way through the ground. A gentle breeze
brought the smell of flowers.

And then Kevin, as if waking from a dream, blinked his eyes slowly and gave a small grin. "I like you, too, Donna," he said in a quiet voice.

"Hurrah!" cried all the Care Bears together.

"We've broken Coldheart's spell," said Friend Bear.

"Coldheart was wrong. People still do want to share their feelings. I'm so glad!" Love-a-lot said.

"Drat!" snarled Coldheart as he scuttled away into the park. "The Care Bears have wrecked my plan. I'll have to come up with something else . . ."

So the Care Bears, Donna and Kevin all went back
to Kevin's house.

When they got to the door, Funshine Bear said,
"Now Kevin, go in there and try to talk out your
problems with your mother and father. It won't be
easy, but we know that you can do it."

"Won't you come with me?" Kevin asked.

"No," said Good Luck Bear as he handed Kevin a four-leaf clover. "But take this for luck and remember that if you ever need us, we'll be around. I promise that we'll think of you and watch you from Care-a-lot."

And they did.

A
Care Bears
Book
PROOF OF PURCHASE